The Little Mermaid

Grosset & Dunlap

Visit **www.strawberryshortcake.com** to join the Friendship Club and
redeem your Strawberry Shortcake Berry Points for "berry" fun stuff!

GROSSET & DUNLAP
Published by the Penguin Group
Penguin Group (USA) Inc., 375 Hudson Street, New York, New York 10014, U.S.A.
Penguin Group (Canada), 90 Eglinton Avenue East, Toronto, Ontario, Canada M4P 2Y3
(a division of Pearson Penguin Canada Inc.)
Penguin Books Ltd, 80 Strand, London WC2R ORL, England
Penguin Ireland, 25 St Stephen's Green, Dublin 2, Ireland
(a division of Penguin Books Ltd)
Penguin Group (Australia), 250 Camberwell Road, Camberwell, Victoria 3124, Australia
(a division of Pearson Australia Group Pty Ltd)
Penguin Books India Pvt Ltd, 11 Community Centre, Panchsheel Park, New Delhi - 110 017, India
Penguin Group (NZ), Cnr Airborne and Rosedale Roads, Albany, Auckland 1310, New Zealand
(a division of Pearson New Zealand Ltd)
Penguin Books (South Africa) (Pty) Ltd, 24 Sturdee Avenue, Rosebank, Johannesburg 2196, South Africa

Penguin Books Ltd, Registered Offices:
80 Strand, London WC2R ORL, England

Library of Congress Cataloging-in-Publication Data

Bryant, Megan E.
The little mermaid / by Megan E. Bryant ; illustrated by Tonja and John Huxtable.
p. cm. — (Berry fairy tales)
"Strawberry Shortcake."
Summary: An adaptation of the traditional tale of a mermaid who falls in love
with a human, featuring Strawberry Shortcake and her friends as the various characters.
ISBN 0-448-44346-5
[1. Fairy tales. 2. Mermaids—Fiction.] I. Huxtable, Tonja, ill. II. Huxtable, John, ill. III. Andersen, H.C.
(Hans Christian), 1805-1875. Lille havfrue. English. IV. Title. V. Series.
PZ8.B8425Lit 2006
[E]—dc22
2005024808

10 9 8 7 6 5 4 3 2 1

Berry Fairy Tales

The Little Mermaid

By Megan E. Bryant

Illustrated by Tonja and John Huxtable

Grosset & Dunlap

Once upon a time, Strawberry Shortcake and her friends spent the day at Seaberry Beach.

"Sometimes I think Seaberry Beach is the berry best place in the whole wide world!" Strawberry exclaimed. "I wish I could stay here all the time."

"What about your berry patch?" asked Orange Blossom. "Strawberries can't grow in the sand."

"And wouldn't you miss Strawberryland?" added Blueberry Muffin.

"Well, sure," Strawberry replied. "But Seaberry Beach has soft, sandy beaches and pretty tropical flowers and seashells that sound like the ocean! And there are seaberries in the lagoon, and I bet mermaids live there, too. That's why I wish I never had to leave."

Strawberry closed her eyes and listened to the sound of the waves washing onto the shore. She began to imagine a world deep in the ocean . . .

. . . where there was an enchanted castle under the sea. Hidden behind twisting strands of seaweed and lacy curtains of coral, the sea castle was home to four special mermaid friends—Seastar, Coral, Shell, and Pearlberry. The mermaids loved living beneath the sea—except for Pearlberry.

"Wouldn't it be wonderful to be a human?" Pearlberry sighed dreamily. "To live on land? To walk and run and play on the shore?"

"Pearlberry, silly, you know mermaids can't go to the shore!" Seastar exclaimed.

"Besides, if you lived on land, everyone in the ocean would miss you," Shell said gently. "Especially us."

"I know," Pearlberry said softly. "I would miss you, too." But that didn't stop her from wishing she could live above the sea.

One summer evening, just after the sun had set, a shadow crossed the ocean floor. Pearlberry looked up as a small boat passed overhead.

"I've always wanted to swim beside a boat!" exclaimed Pearlberry. With a flick of her tail, Pearlberry swam up to the boat. In the glow of the full moon, she saw a boy standing on the deck, playing a pipe. "How beautiful!" Pearlberry whispered as she hid in the shadows of clouds crossing the sky.

Suddenly, a bolt of lightning ripped through the night. Thunder crashed as large raindrops pelted the choppy sea. It was a summer squall! A giant wave smashed into the boat, splintering it into hundreds of pieces. The boy was thrown into the sea!

Oh, no! thought Pearlberry. *Humans can't live underwater. The boy will drown unless I can save him!*

Pearlberry swam to the boy as quickly as she could and hooked her arm around his chest. The rough waves made swimming difficult even for Pearlberry, but soon she was able to drag the boy onto the sand.

This is wonderful, Pearlberry thought happily. *Being on land is even better than I dreamed it would be!*

Pearlberry listened to all the new sounds around her—the wind blowing through the grass, the birds twittering in the trees, and the ponies gently whinnying. But beneath it all, there was something she had been hearing for her whole life: the familiar song of the waves crashing on the shore.

That night, Pearlberry was berry tired from her busy day. But try as she might, she couldn't fall asleep. The sounds of the sea rang in her ears.

Pearlberry slipped out of bed and tiptoed onto the balcony. Suddenly, she longed for her home in the ocean. "What have I done?" she asked as a tear slipped down her face. "I didn't even get to say good-bye to my friends! And now I can never go back!"

Then Pearlberry remembered something—Prince Huckleberry had said she was a great swimmer! "I've spent my whole life swimming," Pearlberry said firmly. "Surely I can swim to see my friends once more!"

Pearlberry ran to the shore and dove into the ocean. She kicked and kicked her legs—but it was not the same as swimming with her powerful mermaid tail.

The farther Pearlberry swam, the rougher the waves became. "Help!" she cried as a wave crashed over her head. "I'm sinking!"

Suddenly there was a warm glow of light, and Pearlberry found herself being carried to a rock jutting out of the sea. Once again, the Berry Fairy was by her side.

"Oh, Pearlberry," the Berry Fairy said sadly. "I tried to warn you. Were you not certain about becoming a human?"

"I was—I am—I don't know!" Pearlberry said. "Being on land is what I've always wanted—but I feel homesick for the sea."

"Are you alive?" Pearlberry whispered. "Please be alive!"

A girl came running down the shore, crying, "Huckleberry! Huckleberry!"
The boy coughed and gasped for air, just as Pearlberry slipped behind a rock.
She watched as the boy, Huckleberry, slowly sat up. She was very proud to
have saved him—and now she wanted to stay on land more than she ever had
before.

"I wish I could be a human!" Pearlberry said sadly as a sob caught in her throat. "I don't want to go under the sea ever again!"

Then a small, shimmering light caught Pearlberry's eye. "You don't *have* to go back," a tiny voice said.

It was a Berry Fairy!

"What—what do you mean?" asked Pearlberry.

"You saved the life of a human tonight," the Berry Fairy replied. "You are entitled to one wish—but only one wish. Be certain that your heart truly desires it, for once the wish is granted, it cannot be undone."

"I know exactly what I want!" Pearlberry exclaimed. "I want to live on land, like a human."

A flash of light streaked across Pearlberry's tail. She looked down—and saw two strong legs. Then a swirl of sparkles surrounded Pearlberry, and she found herself wearing a dress as soft and shimmery as sea spray.

Pearlberry gasped. "Oh, thank you, Berry Fairy!" she said. "This is a dream come true."

But the Berry Fairy had disappeared, leaving Pearlberry all alone—except for the two human children, who were walking away from her.

"W-wait!" Pearlberry called as she tried to stand on her new legs. "Please wait!"

Huckleberry turned around. "Look, Blueberry!" he said. "There she is—the girl who saved me!"

Huckleberry and Blueberry ran to Pearlberry. "I thought you said a mermaid saved you," teased Blueberry.

"I must have imagined it," Huckleberry replied, shaking his head. He turned to Pearlberry. "You're a great swimmer! I'm Prince Huckleberry, and this is my sister, Princess Blueberry. What's your name?"

"I'm Pearlberry," she replied.

"And you're a hero!" exclaimed Princess Blueberry. "You must come with us to the castle. You saved the prince's life!"

Pearlberry smiled at her new friends. "Is—is it far?" she asked shyly. "I'm a little shaky on my feet."

"Don't worry," Prince Huckleberry replied as he took Pearlberry's arm. "We can help you. That's what friends are for, after all!"

In the morning, Princess Blueberry gently woke Pearlberry. "Wake up, sleepyhead!" she said. "Huck and I have planned a berry fun day."

Pearlberry grinned. "I don't want to miss a thing!"

Princess Blueberry and Prince Huckleberry introduced Pearlberry to the pretty ponies in the castle stable, and then taught her how to ride one. The three friends galloped out to a meadow of clover and wildflowers, where they had a picnic of sandwiches, strawberries, and teacakes. Pearlberry couldn't wait to try each new food!

"Pearlberry, don't you know how lucky you are?" the Berry Fairy asked kindly. "Your heart is big enough to love two places at once. You can carry your home in your heart wherever you go."

"Then why do I feel so sad?" Pearlberry asked. "I wish I'd stayed in the sea."

"I can't undo the wish you made," replied the Berry Fairy. "But I can do this: Each month, when the full moon glows in the night sky, you will become a mermaid again. You may swim out to sea and visit your mermaid friends."

And so it was: Pearlberry stayed on the shore, where she lived in the castle with Prince Huckleberry and Princess Blueberry. Each day the three friends explored the meadows and the woods; they danced and skipped and played, enjoying all the wonders of the land.

But once a month, when the reflection of the full moon gleamed like a pearl on the sea, Pearlberry slipped back into the water. With her strong tail and shiny fins, the little mermaid returned once more to visit her home beneath the sea.

Strawberry Shortcake wiggled her toes in the warm sand as she watched the setting sun sink lower in the sky. "Come on, everybody," she called out. "It's getting late. Time to go home."

"Aww, come on, Strawberry!" said Huck. "Let's stay for just a few more minutes."

"Yeah!" added Angel Cake. "Besides, I thought you wanted to stay at Seaberry Beach *forever*."

Strawberry grinned at her friends. "Not if that means leaving my home—and all of you!" she replied. "We can come back and visit Seaberry Beach another day."

That's exactly what they did—and they lived happily ever after!